Dreamers in a Drift State
by Bobby Housel

D1519493

In the pages that follow you will find eleven short stories and twenty-one poems written by myself, Bobby Housel, over the period of 2016 to 2022. Additionally, you'll find a few of my favorite artistic photographs that I've captured during these years.

These stories and poems attempt to pen the everyday trials of a wide assortment of individuals. I often describe reading my work as similar to being a "fly on the wall," observing a brief moment of another's life. You're thrown into the midst of a private moment, you observe, and then it's over. That's it. Real, raw, and hopefully, it gives you another lens to see the world.

I am damn lucky. I grew up in the suburbs of Cleveland, Ohio with the white picket fence and the big backyard. Two loving parents, private school - I had it all. But what I also had, was a bubble. I had to venture outside the walls of the bubble I was living in to find the stories I was looking to tell. To me, there's something a lot more real about life when you don't have a safety net, when you're putting something, perhaps everything, on the line every day.

I firmly believe we learn the most about ourselves and life when we make ourselves uncomfortable, when we are completely lost without any sense of which way is up. Growing up, writing was a way for me to empathize - it was a way for me to escape my bubble. I was chasing experiences. I was hunting for uncomfortable moments. Put simply, I was chasing new lenses to see the world - a way for me to connect with more than just the world I had been brought up in.

I'm so appreciative of you taking the time to read my work. This collection has been written, revised, and rewritten more times than I can count. I hope you enjoy.

One more note - I want to thank my friend Noah Jacobs for inspiring me to take all my work and compile it into this collection. Simply put, without him this book wouldn't exist. I'd also like to thank and credit "Out of the Dark Typefaces" for the use of their font, "Rauschen" in the creation of my front and back covers.

Cheers,

Billy Housel

This collection is dedicated to the crazy ones, the yes sayers, the true adventurers and storytellers.

"Not until we are lost do we begin to understand ourselves." -Henry David Thoreau

First Time, Ohio, 2017 (This and following pictures were taken by Bobby Housel)

Table of Contents:

Short Stories

Poems

Short Stories:

Haze, Ohio, 2017

His brain rarely ran blank. When he was young, he had trouble keeping himself present. Suddenly, he'd be hyperventilating, considering how the decision he had just made would fail him in fifteen years. He tried to slow things down in his head, keep things from spinning out of control. The rare days when his brain could run blank were bliss.

Now he was seventy-six and newly retired. A year ago, he had finally stepped down as the Chief Operating Officer of some firm in New York. He took his severance package and bought a farm in Arkansas. He figured there wouldn't be many operating officers in Arkansas.

It was an unseasonably warm day for late fall, summer fighting for its last moments of relevancy before the leaves and the weather turned. The sun was coming down and he sat in a light brown wooden rocking chair. It had some nicks in it and squeaked on its rotations backwards.

In the rocking chair to his left sat his first, and only, wife. She was sipping lukewarm tea. Her chair did not squeak.

The property sat on forty acres and it made it hard to hear noise coming from neighbors or the road. Sometimes he could hear the birds at night. He couldn't hear anything that afternoon, except for the squeaking of the rocking chair.

His grandchildren were visiting that weekend. He could see them in the distance running around, enjoying the forty acres of grasslands.

His grandson was nearing twelve. The two of them had sorted through the farm's barn earlier that

13

day. It was a mix of his and the previous owner's collection of random oddities. The barn housed the stuff that didn't deserve to get thrown away but had no real place anywhere else.

His grandson enjoyed searching through all the junk. The boy was fascinated by all the antiques beginning to rust or mold.

Underneath a tractor, one of the few newer things in the barn, the twelve-year-old had found a hammock. He pulled it out and dusted it off as he looked up to his grandfather for approval. With a nod and a quiet muttering of "take good care of it," the boy was off, running back to the grassy hills of the farm

Soon he was attempting to tie the thing up as his grandfather watched on from the porch.

His mind still didn't go blank often. But the farm was helping. The rocking chair helped too, and in a strange way, so did the squeaking. Beauty in the monotony - wildness in the simplicity. When he let his mind relax, he drifted into the past. Today, he was back in the front seat of his first car, a 1963 black Saab. His second real girlfriend was in the passenger seat.

It was one of those rainy, humid, end of summer days. He was seventeen. She was nineteen. They had decided to go for a drive before the rain settled in.

They had been driving for a while. The rain was lightening up and the two were lost, as was the plan.

The rain finally stopped, but the sky remained bleak. The radio had lost signal and was radiating static. He spotted something familiar up ahead - a large sign shaped like a canoe read:

"Adventure Waterland
Water and Amusement Park
Next Right"

The gates to the park were open. The booth at the gate was empty and the lights were off. The Saab cruised into the parking lot and the newly official boyfriend and girlfriend headed inside under a light mist.

The park had been left completely unlocked. It was eerie, but welcoming, almost as if someone had left it open for the two of them. He took the girl, two years his elder, by the hand, and they walked into the park.

She wore her long blonde hair in a messy fashion. It wasn't ideal for adventures like this. It liked to cover her eyes and it stayed damp when it got wet. She was tall, damn near taller than he was. She thought a lot, deeply, about a lot of things. She always had something on her mind when they drove around together. She was curious and read books no one assigned to her. Her cats really liked her. She was confused by what she wanted from life, and she'd tell him that. She did know she liked spending time with him. She didn't tell him that. They went to coffee shops and museums and reveled in rainy days spent together.

They were adventurers.

~~~

They found themselves in a paddle boat in a small pond adjacent to the waterslides. The slides, unfortunately, had been turned off, leaving them a hollow metal that was beginning to rust. The rain was coming down harder and they were taking turns using the foot pedals to propel the small plastic craft around the pond.

Following their second lap around the pond, they returned to the Saab and began retracing their turns to find their way home. The countryside felt empty. With few cars on the road and speckles of dark houses in the distance, the place emanated a sense of calm complacency.

His parents were gone for the weekend, so they decided to stop at his place. Decidedly hungry after two laps around a pond in a paddle boat in the rain in an unlocked waterpark, they put water on the stove for pasta.

He wondered what she had thought when he suggested they stop by his vacant house. It was a large home and felt empty with only two people in it. Set on ten acres, it had trees surrounding the entire yard and the privacy that came with them. Large windows covered the back of the house and offered a look into the backyard, which led up to a forested ravine.

He was a virgin. So was she. He wasn't sure if either of them were ready.

As they had made a custom of doing that summer, the two set up his hammock. They found the two pines that were relatively close to each other and waited for the water to boil.

The rain had stopped again, yet the sky remained bleak.

They crawled in the hammock together. It was a tight squeeze, but neither minded. They cuddled up and just sat there for a while. They closed their eyes and listened to the wind blowing against the outside of the hammock. He could hear some birds flying overhead in the distance.

It began to rain again, and they tried to pull the edges of the hammock over themselves.

It didn't work.

They were soaking wet. He leaned in and kissed her. She kissed him back. He thought about how this seemed like a scene from a movie. He wasn't sure which one though.

The two kissed and kissed some more. The rain came down harder. They stopped trying to cover themselves with the hammock. Pulling each other closer they both wondered if this was how they would lose their virginity.

It wasn't.

But neither minded. They held each other and kissed until she jumped from the hammock. She started running. He pursued and the two held each other and tilted their heads towards the sky, catching water in their mouths as they ran barefoot through the grass that would soon be covered in a thin layer of rainwater, and in just a few weeks' time, snow.

And at that moment, the water for the pasta boiled over. And his grandson had just figured out how to tie up the hammock between the two trees.

It was eight o'clock, and it was time for the late shift workers to punch in. Denise parked the faded emerald green Toyota behind the gas station. A white Cadillac, likely one of her co-workers, ripped out of the parking lot as she exited her vehicle and made her way for the backdoor. She put in a piece of gum, put on her black square rimmed glasses, and clipped on a name tag as she walked through the backdoor of the gas station. The mint-flavored gum popped repetitively as she changed out of her red hunting boots and into her Nikes. She wore a white collared polo with a pair of black jeans with unintentional holes in them. She was a pretty girl, but played it down.

The store was empty, and the only sound was the electric static emanating from the wall of refrigerators. Whoever worked the prior shift had left early. Denise typed in her six-digit username and five-letter password to confirm the start of her shift.

Brian, her co-worker, had called off a few hours earlier, alleging a terrible stomach flu. Does she buy this? Probably not. Regardless, Denise was the only one working the late shift that night.

She hopped on top of the counter and peered into the glass case that housed the tobacco products. Everything had been stocked and cleaned, leaving Denise already bored and with nothing to do.

She grabbed one of the white-grape flavored cigarillos out of the case and struggled to light it with the white lighter she found underneath the counter. She stood up on top of the counter to stick a piece of duct tape over the smoke detector above the register. She wasn't a big smoker, but found herself smoking when she had nothing else to do. Smoking used to irritate her; in fact, she had ridiculed her father for it. Back then she couldn't stand the smoke; now she just dealt with it — a byproduct of the buzz.

She peered out of the plexiglass windows into the darkness. The four pumps were illuminated by the ancient, decaying white-yellow lights dangling from the overhang. A few of the wires attaching them to the overhang had snapped, leaving them practically begging to fall. Beyond the gas pumps was Route 404, the once superhighway of Missouri, now hardly used due to the recent construction of a cross-state turnpike. There were no stores, houses, or people within a five-mile radius of the gas station — only farmland. She doubted there would be a single customer all night.

As the end of the cigarillo began to shrivel, Denise hopped off the counter and slouched back in the chair behind the register. Buzzed, she closed her eyes and drifted off into a nicotine-lulled nap.

She was not really sleeping though; she was rather involuntarily playing back the memories of her twenty-two-year-old life like a film in her head. She found herself having these flashbacks more and more when there was nothing to do during the late shifts. They were uncontrollable; they couldn't be stopped once they began. The memories showed her a film she did not want to see, a film she could not escape. The fights, the addictions, the tears, the failed relationships, and the beatings raced around her mind. These were the inevitable circumstances that had led her to this moment, sitting behind the register of a gas station at one o'clock in the morning. She saw herself getting thrown out of high school. Then the screen

20

went black and shifted to the end of her first relationship.

She saw a former, older, abusive boyfriend stumbling around before taking a swing at her and declaring their relationship over. Then she was watching herself mercilessly beating up her former best friend. Then the grand finale: an intoxicated and intensely frightening father pushing Denise up against the wall and running his slippery tongue down the side of her face and into the corner of her mouth.

Her aspirations had died behind that cash register.

Her eyes shot open. She had seen enough. She slid her phone out from her pocket to check the time. Only 2:30 am - another three and a half hours of doing absolutely nothing.

Suddenly she had something to do. The corded phone attached to the wall next to the tobacco case began to ring. She picked up the phone and put it to her ear.

"Hello, this is Denise."

"Hey, slut. How's pumping gas? You're in for a great shift tonight," the voice cooed on the other end of the receiver.

The line went dead, and Denise put the phone back on the wall. She wished that this phone call alarmed her more. At this point in her life, she had received so many threats and been called so many things. These empty words no longer affected her.

The voice had been masculine, but other than that, Denise had been given no clues as to who had called. She didn't feel like trying to determine who might have wanted to harm her. What was the point? She pulled out her phone hoping for notifications of any kind, but was only confronted with an Amber Alert and the time. She untangled and plugged in the crumpled-up ear buds from her jeans' pocket and put her favorite playlist on shuffle. She tried to go back to sleep.

Instead of being confronted with memories or nightmares, Denise saw utter nothingness as a black void gobbled up her reality. The state of calm brought a well-needed break. She was asleep for almost two hours before she was brought back to consciousness by the smell of an electrically charged smoke. It smelled like a backed-up printer had caught fire.

Denise's body grew warm as she caught the scent of the acrid odor. She fell out of her chair and woke up on the ground of a burning store. She immediately began coughing.

In a state of panic, she got up and ran out the back door, dodging the flames that now engulfed the store. The gas pumps were intact, but the inside of the store was quickly disintegrating.

The fire truck came quickly, and within ten minutes of its arrival, the fire was out. The fire didn't have enough time to spread to the gas tanks or destroy the structure of the building, but it had destroyed almost everything on the inside, except Denise. Her boss arrived at the store and questioned her as to how this could have happened. She had no good response, as she had been sleeping. He made it clear he wanted to fire her but spared her for the time being. With a scowl, he told her to go home.

As she approached the old Toyota, she saw red spray paint covering the windshield. The word "worthless" had been painted onto her car in all caps.

Denise got in the car and drove home as the sun began to rise.

The blue Mustang groaned as he pushed in the clutch and moved the gear shifter into neutral. He pulled the keys out of the ignition and tossed them into the cup holder. It had just begun to rain, and the sky was darkening. It was one of those nights in the summer when the heat was rising off the road and the headlights crashed through the fog. Steam crept up off the asphalt as the rain hit the ground. He rolled down the driver's side window just to smell it.

Rain trickled through the gap in the window and splattered on his grey sweatpants. He left the window open. It felt good. He reached for the faded blue Yankees hat that rested on top of his head. He took it down and examined it. The wear looked good, almost as if it had been the original design. Did that mean he was old? He dismissed the thought.

He bent the brim a bit more and tapped the cap against the side of his head a few times. A deep sigh came out of his mouth as he reached for the door. He pushed it open and stepped onto his former driveway. It began to rain harder. He slammed the car door and moved towards the house's entrance.

What happened next happened fast, like it did every last Thursday of the month. Door opens. Laura appears. Laura yells for Ricky, telling him dad is here. Ricky comes running. Ricky embraces him. Dad hugs back. The door shuts. Laura disappears. Like clockwork.

Dad walked back to the car. Ricky lifted his head to the sky and tilted it back, catching the rain as he ran. By the time he got to the passenger door, his mouth overflowed with rainwater. His mother didn't let him ride in the front seat. Dad didn't get preoccupied with these things. Ricky, in the front seat alongside dad, had already begun dripping rainwater onto the leather of the Mustang.

Ricky had red hair and was not very bright for his age. Was he five or six? Fuck, Dad had forgotten. Ricky liked monster trucks and toys that sparkled. He was quiet, probably due to the speech impediment that both parents had ignored. When he did talk, he chose his words carefully, tripping over words that had the letter 'r' in them. Wicky.

Dad was fifty something and tired. God, was he tired. He was twice divorced and no longer interested in picking up the easy piece of ass he could find at the bars he frequented. After about the fifth drink, he always told the bartender he felt as if he had lived three lifetimes. Interested more in their tips than how many lifetimes their clients had lived, the bartenders usually nodded and came back with another drink.

He went by "Matt." This was his preferred name, not his real name. He would've changed his name, legally, if he had the money. He worked as a contractor, fixing whatever he could convince people he knew how to fix. He liked room temperature beer and silence. He, too, chose his words carefully.

Matt looked over his shoulder as he backed out of the driveway. Ricky ran his Grave Digger monster truck alongside the armrest of the passenger door, animating its motions with sound effects as Grave Digger flipped and tumbled onto the ground.

Matt made three lefts and got on the highway heading towards Olympia. He reclined his seat slightly and let out another sigh as he reached once again for the Yankees hat. He took it off and ran his fingers

26

through his thick brown hair. The roots were beginning to grey. He leaned forward and put the steering wheel between his knees as he pushed his hair back with his left hand and put the hat on with his right. He reached for the radio, trying to tune into a station, but could only find static. He turned the radio off and focused on the sound of the rain on the car's hood instead of the sounds of Grave Digger.

After about forty minutes on the highway, Matt turned off onto exit 203. The exit's blue sign that was supposed to be advertising gas, food, and attractions, was blank. He made a right and the road was suddenly surrounded by tall pine trees. About a mile down, a green sign was splattered with mud, making the words "Doc's Family Motel, 3 Miles Ahead" barely legible.

In three miles, Matt pulled the Mustang into the motel's parking lot and into the now familiar spot in front of unit seven. He peered into the reception office, but the light was off. It looked like Doc didn't mind waiting another day for his rent.

He looked over to the passenger seat and Ricky looked back, momentarily pausing Grave Digger's adventures.

They got out of the car and walked up to unit seven. It was still raining.

Matt pulled the key out from his sweatpants and opened the door. Ricky ran inside and jumped on Matt's bed, Grave Digger in hand. Matt turned on the lamp and turned the heat on the thermostat up. He looked around the room. There was a wooden desk with some dents in it and a black microwave on top, one twin bed with a small, plastic nightstand to its right, and a sink with green stains in its basin at the end of the room. To the right of the sink was a shower with no shower curtain and a toilet that had a habit of overflowing.

Ricky drove Grave Digger across the bed, seemingly unbothered by the squalor of the place. Matt grabbed an Insta Ramen off the top of the microwave and went to the sink to fill it with water. The water had a metallic taste to it and looked it. He put the cup in the microwave and punched in three minutes, taking a seat in front of the desk.

Matt liked how the rain made the roof of unit seven ping. The roof was some kind of metal and rang beautifully when the water fell from the sky. After a moment, the beeping of the microwave took Matt away from his trance. He got the cup out and looked around for a spoon he knew he didn't own. He handed the cup, with no spoon, to Ricky as Grave Digger dove into the comforter.

After finishing the ramen with his hands, Ricky resumed playing with the only toy his mother let him bring for the weekend. Ricky liked having his own bed when he was with his dad; he didn't have to share with mom like when he was back home.

After a few more flips and jumps with Grave Digger, Ricky set the toy on the nightstand next to the empty ramen cup and pulled down the comforter. He pulled the sheets up over his head and curled up with the two paper thin pillows. He passed out quickly.

Matt was, once again, examining his hat when he heard Ricky start to snore. He took the Yankees hat and set it upside down next to the microwave.

He got up and walked over to the sink, turning the right knob clockwise, hoping for hot water. After a minute, he knew he would be settling for cold. Cupping the water with his hands, he splashed it onto his cheeks. He splashed it onto his forehead and into his eyes. The water was freezing; it made his skin tingle. The water dripped off his stubble and into the sink. He reached for the grimy towel that he hadn't washed in weeks and rubbed his face dry.

He glanced at Ricky. The boy was out cold. Matt took the comforter off the end of the bed and set it on the floor next to the wooden desk. He returned to the bottom of the bed and got onto his knees. He lifted the bed skirt and tilted his head sideways as he leaned onto his left forearm so he could see under the bed frame. His right arm was fully extended under the bed, fumbling around in search of the plastic bag. With some struggle, he managed to grip the plastic and pull it out from under the bed. He got back onto his knees and stood up.

Ricky had sat up in bed and was staring at his father at the foot of the bed. Matt stared back, plastic bag in hand. Neither sure what the other was thinking, Ricky laid back down and pulled the cover back over his head.

Matt laid down on the floor and pulled the comforter over his head too. His feet stuck out from the bottom of the comforter. He was glad he had turned the heat up.

He sat up and unzipped the plastic bag. He pulled off his green long sleeve t-shirt and tossed it onto the desk alongside the Yankees hat. His left forearm was bruised. There were six pinpoint holes scattered around his veins.

What happened next happened fast. He pulled the syringe out of the plastic bag. He rubbed the needle on the comforter. He reached back into the bag and retrieved the vial. He inserted the needle into the

29

vial and pulled back the head of the syringe. He grabbed a purple, rubber cord out of the bag and tied it tightly around his forearm, balancing the syringe in his lap. He resealed the vial and put it back in the bag. Scouring his forearm, he found a spot not already bloodied or bruised and stuck the needle in, pushing the head of the syringe to empty its contents into his body. He removed the needle, placed it in the bag, untied the rubber cord, placed it too in the bag, closed the bag, and slid it across the carpet and back under the bed. Like clockwork.

He used the crook of his left arm as a pillow as he began to feel tired. It was a big dose. He didn't plan on waking up. He figured Doc would come looking for his rent and find him and Ricky in the morning. He would then call Laura and have her come pick up Ricky. Then someone from the morgue could come pick up Matt.

What happened next happened fast. Sun was peering through the window of that cheap motel room. A set of rubber wheels drove across a nose and a forehead. Grave Digger was cruising across Matt's face. Matt did not respond. Grave Digger went down the neck and across the chest. Matt didn't move. Ricky kicked his father in the abdomen. Matt gasped and opened his eyes, still in a haze, somewhere far away. Ricky looked into his father's eyes.

"I'm hungry."

Alone in the Rain

It was a stormy summer night at a roadside diner in rural Alabama. It was the kind of night when families lost power at their homes in the suburbs and huddled together under candlelight. I sat at the counter, pensive, drained. The cherry red leather of my high-top seat was ripping, exposing the yellow foam inside. I could hear the rainwater rolling off the metal roof into the gutters of the small diner. Cara, my waitress, scurried back to replenish my coffee. She asked if I was okay, and I nodded, lying, without lifting my eyes.

The coffee was cold.

The bags under my eyes must have been obvious. It had been twenty days since I left home. My phone sat at the bottom of a roadside creek some hundred miles north of where I was now. It was undoubtedly filled with missed calls from my wife and daughters. Even when I had had my phone, there was no reaching me; I was off the grid mentally, just as much as I was physically.

I sipped on the strongly brewed coffee and slowly lifted my head up from my death stare at the counter. I realized I was the only customer in the diner. Other than the ticking of the ancient analog clock hanging on the wall, the room was silent. Cara stood in the kitchen filing her nails as she anxiously awaited my departure.

I reached into my torn brown wallet and tossed four dollars onto the counter. I caught a glimpse of a picture of my daughters that I kept folded in my wallet. As I went to put the wallet back into my jeans' pocket, my eyes averted. I tossed the picture onto the counter alongside the four dollars. I walked to the door without making a noise. The bells on the door interrupted the silence and I faintly heard Cara attempt to bid me farewell.

The rain had grown louder and pounded on the hood of my black Nissan. The flimsy yellow raincoat I wore did little to protect me from the storm. The car door stuck briefly before I yanked it open and collapsed into the driver's seat.

The car rumbled to a start after one failed attempt at igniting the old and unreliable engine. The radio crackled back to life, but only emitted a low static buzz.

I wanted to turn my car around and go home, but I knew it was too late. I couldn't face my family. This was for the best. Despite their prayers, they would come to realize they were better off without me.

I let the static of the radio mingle with the pouring rain to create a mind-numbing song. I drove faster than I should have. An hour of driving passed and I did not see a single car on that rural road in southern Alabama. I saw only the dark, muddled rainwater reflecting on the hood of the Nissan.

I pulled off at a rest stop and parked the car outside the bathrooms. I grabbed my toothbrush and deodorant from the trunk and went to brush my teeth. I had grown accustomed to the grime of rest stop bathroom water. The sink didn't work, so I was left to rinse out the toothpaste with my own spit. After rubbing deodorant all over my body, I turned back to my car for what I assumed would be another restless night's sleep stretched out in the backseat. On my way I saw a sleeping homeless man slumped against the wall inside the rest stop. His beard was dirty and made him look a lot older than he actually was. His fingernails had browned under the tips and his ripped green jacket was wrapped around him tightly.

I deposited the toothbrush and deodorant into my trunk. I let the cold rainwater run down my neck and drench my only set of clothes. My head tilted back, I opened my mouth and let the water swish in and out.

I walked back to the homeless man and set my keys and wallet next to him. I knew they wouldn't help him, but I knew they wouldn't help me, either. I turned away and walked out of the rest stop, back into the downpour, and out into the darkness.

Moonlight

It was one of those nights when the cold couldn't bother me. I wasn't really there.

The rounded metallic roof of my car shimmered under the soft moonlight. The metal curved inwards under the weight of my body.

I inhaled deeply, sucking in the icy winter air. I felt my phone vibrate; I ignored it. Nothing it could have said was worth distracting myself.

The light descended from the long-abandoned billboard, its yellow tentacles crawling up just short of my car. Only two of the three floodlights above the billboard were still in operating condition. The light produced a buzzing noise just loud enough to disrupt the winter night's silence.

I reached out to grab her hand, my eyes closed. I was brought back to reality when I felt its absence. It hadn't been there for years.

I let my imagination take me back to our home. I saw our son outside, and I saw her lying on a lawn chair, just close enough to keep a watchful eye. It was a mundane moment; I couldn't understand why I was remembering it. It was just a quiet Sunday that had unfolded week after week. I couldn't remember why I was sitting on my car under a billboard in the middle of winter. I couldn't remember what I had done before I had driven out here. How long had I been here?

I opened my eyes. The stars were glowing. I looked up in the sky, unable to identify any constellations. I had always been terrible at recognizing them, so we used to make up our own. Small flakes of snow began to fall, illuminated by the wavering yellow light.

A group of barely visible stars caught my eye. I imagined them to be a spider's web. I saw the spider approach its ensnared prey: a fly. Suddenly a shooting star darted left; the fly was not dead yet.

I saw the fly squirm weakly, seemingly accepting its fate. The spider inched closer. The fly shivered once more. Maybe it was cold. Maybe it was scared. One thing was clear: it was alone.

As the spider opened its pincers, the sky glowed a little brighter. Only it was still too early to say who was the spider and who was the fly.

Dreamers in a Drift State

Glowing White-Yellow Spheres dangle from the ceiling, their diameter maybe ten or so inches across. A Grill is grilling some cheap, bought in bulk onions somewhere off in the kitchen. Utensils cast in plastic clink as they reunite following a long shower. Customers trickle in and trickle out, without much purpose. They seem to drift. Nowhere much to go. Chitter chatter lingers in the air.

"How are you?"

"What can I get for you?"

"Did you see the game?"

"What brings you here?"

"Is that all?"

"Good. Tea. I didn't. Nothing really. Yes."

I tell them I'm a writer, here to write, or something. I figure if they believe it, maybe I'll start to, too. They're curious, probing me. I don't have much for them.

They're kind, at least, kind to those that treat them like humans. To be treated like a human person, what an honor. Flattering, really.

It goes quiet again. The drifters must have decided to drift on out. Drift on out to somewhere else where drifters are welcome. Now we, or rather me, get a chance to enjoy this little beauty's symphony. Half a dozen Fans. A semi lively stretch of Back Road outside, Route 36, I think. A Gurgling Coffee Maker that's seen better decades. And a Jukebox, hungry, that hasn't been fed in many years. Instead of songs, it plays this low static buzz, inaudible to all those that aren't listening for it.

The tea is getting cold. She asks if I want another. She's kind. Her eyes prove it. She won't charge me for more than one. I oblige, "Sure," I say. "Any other flavors?"

"Lavender," she says. I know it will smell better than it tastes. I nod.

A bit of it drips onto my sleeve. A souvenir! I smell where it dribbled down. It didn't leave any scent.

There's a Clock on the wall. It's way off. That seems appropriate. This place is open twenty-four hours, I'm told. A clock doesn't actually seem so important. I suppose that's why it's in the back right corner.

Nothing much is going on outside. Old Route 36 disappoints yet again. The Traffic Lights haven't turned off yet, though. They still change from green, to yellow, to red. I hate it when they start flashing yellow at night instead of circling through the three-color cycle. It's ridiculous. Only one color instead of three? I hate it.

A few Flags across the street are still dancing, now somewhat limply. Too bad they can't hear the Jukebox. Some leftover Christmas Lights are fighting for relevancy in the first week of February. And would you look at that! The boys upstairs decided to let some of the white stuff flutter down. Great news. And the Traffic Lights are still changing and the Jukebox still mumbling its electric buzz. This is great. Even the Christmas Lights rejoice in their newfound relevancy. Snow!

It drifts down for a while, in no rush, really. It's piling up a bit. There's chatter in the kitchen about a storm.

"How will we get home?"

"How are the roads?"

"Are you gonna make it okay?"

"You think the trucks are out plowing?"

"Those Christmas Lights look pretty in the snow."

Point Christmas Lights. Relevancy restored. Too bad they are too far away to hear the compliment.

I don't drive. The white stuff and I will commingle on my walk home. I like it better that way. Touching it, feeling it melt. I imagine it prefers it that way, too. I know the Christmas Lights are with me on this one. They melt the white stuff real good with their heat and all.

I get up to go to the bathroom. Some guy grunts as he walks out. It's clean. Probably cleaner than it need be. I rinse off my hands and splash some water on my face. I unzip the fly to my pants and let some of the tea out. I head back to the table, not washing my hands on the way out. I washed them upon entry, after all. Something I heard the Japanese do. I don't know. Maybe I made that up. Maybe that's not true. Maybe that's not Route 36. I don't know. Neither do the Christmas Lights, though. They don't know either.

Another drifter, drifts in. Comments on the snow, doesn't comment on the Christmas Lights. This one feels a bit more lost than the rest. Sober, sure, but plenty lost. He looks to the corner booth, not at me, but at the Jukebox. I can tell he's listening. He drifts on over, pauses, and drifts right into the seat across from me. He doesn't say anything. Orders some tea and queues back in on the melody emanating from the corner. He notices the Glowing White-Yellow Spheres dangling from the ceiling. Glances over to the

39

Silverware. He sips his tea, drops his chin into his chest. He picks his head up, glances at me. I think I recognize him. I notice a stain on his sleeve.

"Have you seen the Christmas Lights?" he asks.

"No."

Bailey wheeled the decrepit white bicycle out of the garage and into the driveway. The back wheel was half deflated, and the white paint was beginning to chip, revealing a dull metallic color. The handlebars were slightly elevated, and the bike was predominantly white with flares of blue. The spokes were a faded crimson and ridden with rust.

Two trading cards stuck out of the spokes, one in the front wheel, and one in the back. The card in the front was John Elway's rookie card; almost nobody had got it when it released. Bailey's dad loved Elway. The card in the back was old and faded, and the athlete could no longer be identified. A brown stain marked where the player used to be.

Bailey pushed his long, light brown hair out of his eyes with the back of his hand. He wore a dark blue, off-brand hoodie with a pair of green ripped jeans. He synched the drawstrings of his hoodie as a gust of wind blew his hair back into his face.

He took a torn rag out of his back pocket and wetted it under the hose. He wiped the frame of the bike down, removing some flaking paint in the process.

Bailey was not allowed to stay out late like his friends. Curfew normally came due at quarter to one. His parents were stricter than most, or at least his dad was. When he was home, he lay in bed for hours trying to fall asleep. 1 AM was when he went to lie down. Two was when the house finally started to quiet down, and the doors stopped slamming. Three was when he finally could fall asleep. He used a towel from his bathroom to block the noise from filtering in under his door. It only muffled it, so he started taking to wrapping his head with two pillows.

After the bike shined to his liking, he stashed it in a bush alongside the house. The house was a small Victorian home. It had three floors and looked like a little church. It was a sea foam green that over the years had darkened in color. The lights were always on in the front windows and the tiles were beginning to fall off the roof.

After covering the bike with leaves and making sure it was out of sight of any of the windows, he returned inside through the back door. The door squeaked behind him as he scampered up the back set of stairs.

His mother was sitting at the kitchen table, smoking. She stirred the cup of coffee in front of her and let the steam rise into her face. Her mascara was running, and she pulled another cigarette out of her purse. Bailey paused and watched her for a moment before he went up the stairs. She didn't hear him, and she kept stirring the cup.

Bailey entered his bedroom and plopped himself onto his bed. He reached under his mattress and felt around for the *Playboy* magazine. After a short struggle he finally grasped it and ripped it out from under the mattress. He flipped through the pages until he found his favorite picture. The woman was blonde and had fierce brown eyes. She was lying down on an elegant rug, completely nude. The background was blurred, but he could make out a fireplace burning behind the model. He stared intently at the picture before moving his right hand into his pants. He quickly beat off and returned the magazine to its hiding spot.

A Denver Broncos clock hung from the right wall of Bailey's room. The clock read 11:10 PM, but he knew it to be exactly one hour and seventeen minutes fast. He swung his feet over the edge of his bed and put on his white, Nike Air Force 1 sneakers. He picked up the walkie-talkie from his bedside table and slipped it into the pocket of his hoodie. He opened his bedroom door, slowly, trying to make as little noise as possible. Perched at the bottom of the stairs, he peered around the corner and saw his mother sitting with her face on top of her hands at the table. He could hear her snoring. He tiptoed through the kitchen and out the front door. His dad's car was not in the driveway, and he knew he was home free. He walked around to the side of the house and retrieved the bicycle from the bush. Pushing off, he turned the bicycle out of his driveway, and into the deserted residential street.

His sweatshirt was rumbling. He took the walkie-talkie out of his pocket and held it to his ear. He had had that walkie-talkie since he was in middle school. All his friends had gotten newer versions or mobiles, but Bailey's father had refused to buy one for him.

"Bailey! Bailey, I repeat, come in. This is Eric," the walkie-talkie declared.

"Yes, this is Bailey. I am en route. Estimated arrival, ten fifteen," he replied.

"Okay, we just got here. I'll tell the boys you are on your way. Over and out."

Bailey put the walkie back into his pocket and began to pedal faster. He hadn't seen the boys in weeks, and adrenaline coursed through his body. He zoomed past homes on the dark side streets. Clouds covered the moon, and it was darker than usual. A light fog had rolled over town from the west.

He flew into the parking lot behind the Walton Hills General Store and docked his bike in the bike rack. Six bikes, in varying conditions, ranging from brand new to complete pieces of shit, were also docked. He flipped out his kickstand and retrieved the walkie from his pocket and raised it to his mouth.

"I'm here."

Bailey heard his own voice echo before Eric could grab his shoulders with two hands from behind.

"Boo!" Eric shouted, as he released Bailey, and his lifelong friend turned around to confront him.

Bailey smiled and reached out his right hand. Eric took his hand and began their special handshake as he pulled Bailey in for a hug.

"Nice to see you man, it's been too long," Eric said.

The rest of the guys emerged from the darkness, five in total. From right to left there was Rick, Vogel, Brian, Anderson, and Dave. One at a time they approached Bailey to do their own handshakes.

"Alright boys it's already ten thirty, let's hit it," Vogel said.

They mounted their bikes and began pedaling. There were no cars on the road. A large cloud shifted off the moon and white light shimmered down through the mid October sky. Halloween was less than two weeks away and the town knew it. Ghosts, pumpkins, and cobwebs dotted front lawns across the town. It was brisk and only getting colder. Walton was one of those towns where nosey people were the norm. Everyone knew everyone and their business. Everyone knew each other's problems too.

Bailey half stood up on his bike to pedal faster to keep up with his friends. His seat was too low and was beginning to dig into his ass. After ten minutes the group of boys stopped alongside a wooded valley and laid their bikes on the grass behind the guardrail off to the right side of the road. They climbed down the steep hill, occasionally cursing as they slipped on the mud. They ran down the last quarter of the hill and grabbed onto a tree every few yards to try and stay on their feet. Anderson reached for a tree with his right hand but missed and fell face first into the side of the hill.

"Shit, what's my mom going to think when she sees this big mud stain?" Anderson complained as Bailey helped him up from the ground.

"Just tell her you shit yourself," Rick giggled.

"Wouldn't be the first time," chimed in Dave, smirking.

After the slow climb down, the boys finally reached the bottom of the hill. Through a patch of trees was their destination. Seven tree stumps formed a semicircle around a small pile of sticks. Dave approached the sticks and began turning them upside down so that the wet side faced the ground and the dry bottoms faced upwards. He swung his green and brown backpack off his back and unzipped the front pocket. He pulled out a white and black striped lighter and held it to the corner of one of the sticks until it began to catch fire. He blew on the flame and let it spread to the other sticks before backing up and taking a seat on his tree stump.

The six other boys were sitting on their stumps and moved their seats forward as the fire grew bigger.

"It's fucking cold as shit out here," Vogel complained.

"Well don't I have the answer to that problem," smiled Eric.

Eric unzipped the big pocket of his backpack and removed fourteen Falstaff beer cans. He dished out two to each of the boys and kept two for himself. In a symphony of "psssh" the cans popped open.

"Nice to have you back with us Bailey," Anderson said as he smiled and looked over to his friend of many years. His voice was tinted with sympathy.

"Nice to be back," Bailey replied as he sipped the beer. "I missed you guys."

Bailey quickly finished the first can and reached down for the second.

"What's new?" Rick asked. "What have you been ditching us for?"

"You know I would never ditch you guys. It's just been kinda rough lately, ya know?" Bailey replied.

Six heads nodded in compliance; they understood not to probe.

They sat in silence, drinking the Falstaff, until Dave broke the silence.

"Anybody want a smoke?" A crooked smile crept over his face as he awaited the answer he always received.

"Dave, nobody wants to smoke your disgusting herbal, unfiltered, ass cigarettes," Eric chuckled.

"Oh well, more for me," Dave said, as he lit the end of the white-brown butt and put the small cylinder into the right corner of his mouth.

Anderson got up and went to go pee against a nearby oak tree.

"Aye Anderson, bring back some more sticks for the fire," ordered Eric. He was the clear leader of the group despite the other six boys' refusal to admit it.

Anderson zipped up his pants and reached down to bring few sticks back to the fire, sticking them in the middle of the still growing flame.

The boys sat around the fire, bullshitting with each other, enjoying the warmth of the flame and each other's company. It felt like the old days.

~~~

Bailey looked down at his watch and saw that it was already nearing one o'clock. Fuck! He used to have the confidence to defy his father, but now he worried. His actions didn't just come back to hurt him anymore.

Bailey stood up and tossed his second beer can to the ground before crushing it under his Nikes and contributing it to the fire.

"Alright boys, I got to get home before my parents find out I left," Bailey said.

"Ah shit, are you sure you gotta leave now?" asked Eric. "What if I were to give you one more of these?" he lifted his unopened second can off the ground and tossed it to Bailey.

Bailey considered it, turning the aluminum can over in his hands.

"I'm sorry," he tossed the can back to Eric.

He was sorry. He was sorry he couldn't keep running away from it.

Bailey went around the half circle of boys, exchanging goodbye handshakes. He walked out of the trees and began his ascent up the muddy hill.

With only two falls, he made it to the top of the hill relatively unscathed. His ripped jeans got a little more ripped and his hoodie only got nicked slightly with some mud. He lifted his bike and carried it around the guardrail and placed its wheels onto the road. He saw that his back tire was lower on air than usual and prayed it made it home without popping. Before getting on his bike, he looked around. He was completely alone. He took a deep breath and let out a long scream as loud as he could. He mounted the bike and pedaled away from his friends.

Slightly buzzed, Bailey weaved on his bike a bit, but managed to keep from tipping over. He hummed the tune of the new Dan Fogelberg song he had heard the other day on the radio. Something about a band leader; he couldn't remember the words, just the instrumental.

After a twenty-minute ride, he turned onto his street. His watch read one fifteen and the lights were off in the windows of the three-story home. A 1965 white Ford Thunderbird was parked in the driveway. There were dirt marks scattered around the wheels and a small dent in the rear fender.

His father was home.

He leaned his bike up against the side of the garage and crept around to the backdoor. Forgetting about the loud creaking the backdoor was prone to, Bailey opened the door and stumbled inside. His mother stirred slightly at the kitchen table but didn't wake. Her head rested in her left elbow next to her pink ashtray. Bailey heard the TV and peered around the corner into the family room. His father sat in his leather reclining chair, watching a re-run of an old Broncos playoff game. He was sipping a brandy and had not heard Bailey enter through the backdoor. Bailey turned back to the kitchen before climbing the stairs that led to his second-floor bedroom. He did not notice his mother's cut lip, or the speckles of blood that stained the kitchen table.

He shut the bedroom door behind him, pushed the noise blocking towel into its space under the door, and kicked his Nikes into the closet. He turned off the overhead light and flicked on his bedside lamp as he collapsed into his small twin bed. He reached under his mattress, fumbling for the Playboy magazine.

In the old days, you didn't have to present your ticket when passing through the security checkpoint. I saw some memorable people when I shined shoes at that airport. I saw some real wackos too. But I'll never forget Bentley. He wasn't a wacko.

I didn't actually know his name. Odds are it wasn't Bentley. I liked to pick names for the people I saw passing through the airport. I don't know what it was, but this guy seemed like a "Bentley;" it suited him.

I shined shoes for years at that airport. It was demanding work. You were always on your knees, just hoping and praying that the hurried travelers stopped to tip you as they got up, shoes looking good as new. Most of the time, they didn't.

The first time I ever saw Bentley was when he sat down to get his loafers shined. I still remember the shoes: light brown wingtip Johnston and Murphy Graysons. They were old and beaten up, but they were classy shoes from a classy era. I said, "Hello." He gave me a nod and plopped himself down in my chair. He was dressed stylishly for an older guy. He sported a light green cashmere sweater and a pair of slightly wrinkled khakis. He wore these stunning Ray-Ban glasses. His emerald eyes were highlighted perfectly by these glasses. I'd never seen eyes like that.

I asked him if he wanted a normal shine and polish. He nodded. He pulled a folded-up newspaper out of his back pocket and never looked up from it.

"That'll be two dollars," I said, as I slung the towel onto my shoulder and put the polish away. He looked up from the newspaper, refolded it, and returned it to his back pocket. He pulled a ten-dollar bill out of the breast pocket of his sweater, and before I could offer him change, he had already begun to walk away.

I didn't see Bentley again for just over a week. This time he sported a colorful pair of shorts and a crisp, linen dress shirt. He had a grey hat on with a logo I did not recognize, and he seemed to tip it to me as he walked past my stand. It was subtle.

He passed my stand, seemingly uninterested in another shine. A newspaper was tucked in the back pocket of his colorful shorts.

I worked all day that shift; I was busy as hell. It was ten o'clock when I finally shut down my stand. By ten, the airport had cleared out, and it was strangely quiet for a Friday night. I packed my things and locked my oils in my chest. As I walked through the busier terminals to get to my car, I saw Bentley sitting in the middle of a crowd of travelers waiting for their planes. He had the newspaper unfolded, right in front of his face. He wasn't reading though. His eyes rested just above the top of the paper and darted back and forth as travelers walked through the terminal. You couldn't miss those eyes behind those glasses.

~~~

Bentley started coming to the airport every day. He never got on any planes to my knowledge. He was always perched at a new location. Sometimes he sat in the food court. Other days he sat in the corner of the waiting areas. Occasionally he sat in the area that overlooked the runway and the aircraft marshallers. He always had that newspaper sitting in front of him, obscuring his face.

He fascinated me. He never said a word to anyone. I occasionally received what I thought was a wink, or a tip of the hat, but it was always hard to tell if he was doing it on purpose.

After about the third month of seeing Bentley sitting throughout the airport, I knew him well. I knew his mannerisms. He took short strides, breathed heavily, always wore his glasses, and appeared to be somewhere around the age of eighty. He always wore the same pair of beaten-up loafers I had polished three months ago. His outfits were dictated by the day of the week. Monday was cashmere sweater day. Tuesday was colorful shorts. Wednesday long sleeve rugby, and so on.

The newspaper he so religiously kept in his back pocket, or in front of his wandering eyes, was the same one from the day I had shined his shoes. Each day he used the same months old newspaper to hide his face.

After six months, I couldn't take it anymore. After closing my stand and locking up my trunk for the night, I went looking for Bentley. First, I checked the food court, then the waiting lobby for Terminal A, and then the area that overlooked the runway. I couldn't find him.

After some persistence, I finally found him sitting in the back corner of the waiting room for the private charters' terminal. He had his usual Friday outfit on, and the newspaper rested in front of his placid face.

I sat down in the seat next to him. He didn't seem to mind that I chose that seat, even though there were only ten other people sitting in the large waiting area.

He didn't turn to look at me. His eyes remained fixed just above the top of his six-month-old newspaper. His breaths were short and relaxed.

Without turning to him, with genuine intrigue, I asked, "Why do you come here?"

He didn't flinch. His breaths remained constant. His eyes remained fixed on the people walking about the terminal. He pulled the newspaper down and turned to me. He pointed his emerald eyes right into mine and said, "I'm studying them."

He lifted the newspaper back in front of his face and redirected his eyes to a group of maintenance workers pushing a cart. After a minute of silence, he suddenly rose to his feet and began to walk away.

He folded the newspaper and returned it to his back pocket. He turned around, looked back at me, and walked backwards for a second. This time I was sure that he gave me a wink. He then turned away and continued walking.

I wasn't satisfied. I tried to follow him, to find the answers I was looking for, but he disappeared around a corner and was gone.

I saw Bentley less frequently after that. Sometimes it'd be once a week, sometimes once every three, but his outfits always stayed consistent with the day of the week, and the newspaper stayed folded in his back pocket.

When he walked by my stand, I knew his winks were intentional.

She sat on that beach, knowing this would be one of the last times she would see her 7-year-old boy.

Their fingers were interwoven, their eyes cast upon the sea. She leaned over, pushing his hair to the side, and gave him a kiss on the forehead. It was half an hour before the sun would set and she could tell that it would be beautiful.

Specks of sand stuck in the boy's brown and curled hair, glistening under the last hour of sunlight. The blues of his eyes shined teal, his lips a rosy pink.

The sun slowly began its descent into the ocean. The sky began to change color and the ocean gobbled up the light. A breeze rolled off the water and sent her hair flying. The breeze smelled of salt. The sky was a watercolor painting.

"I had fun today, Mommy," the boy said quietly as his eyes averted to the sand. He ran his hand over the tops of millions of grains of sand, patting them down.

"Me too, sweetie," she replied, not as warmly as she used to.

She turned away so he couldn't see the look of pain on her face. She didn't want him to know how bad she was hurting.

"Who's going to take care of me when you're in heaven, Mommy?" he asked.

It was quiet for a moment. A half mile offshore a flock of seagulls were jabbering at each other, but neither of them were listening close enough to hear. Both were only present enough to take in a fraction of the beauty unfolding in front of them.

"You know Grandma will, and you know how much she loves you. I'm not going anywhere anytime soon though, I promise."

One of those statements was true.

She forced a smile to reassure him. Seemingly soothed by his mother's lie, the boy let out a sigh and squeezed his mom's hand a bit tighter.

For a while neither of them said anything. The waves cascaded onto the shore, filling the newfound silence. The waves sounded like water shattering glass. In that time, the boy must have somehow known to cherish that moment. He didn't build sandcastles, he didn't play in the water, and he didn't look for seashells. He sat there next to his mother, absorbing her presence. He counted her breaths. Deep inhale; short, wheezy exhale.

A set of wispy clouds rolled in from the west and the setting sun illuminated them. The reddish-yellow light cast down through the clouds speckled the beach. The smell of a midsummer night danced through the dusk.

"Is this what heaven is like?" he asked carefully, unsure of his own question.

Words didn't come, so she just squeezed his hand tighter still and nodded.

The last shards of sunlight dipped under the ocean. Hues of pink clouds remained, the final light of the day. Days like this are difficult days to say goodbye.

Just as it was becoming too dark to see, a flock of birds flew across the ocean in the dying light of that summer day.

"Mommy... why do the birds fly in a line?" the boy asked.

She paused, letting out a shaky breath. A small smile, so small that it could have easily been missed, crept across her face.

"They fly in a line because they are a family. When you fly side by side, wing by wing, hand by hand," she squeezed his hand a little bit tighter, "you are stronger than you could ever be alone."

The mailman should have arrived by now. Martin sat in the rocking chair under the white and blue striped awning of the small colonial home, eyes locked on the mailbox. He ashed his unfiltered cigarette as it began to shrivel. Without taking his eyes off the mailbox, he reached into his pocket to remove another cigarette and match. He dropped the shriveled one into the ashtray and promptly placed the new one between his lips.

The house had been his grandparents', and then his parents', and now his. He was the last one left. His grandparents had built it back in the twenties. It was small and falling apart. It needed work on the exterior and was beginning to show its age. All the houses around it had been torn down and rebuilt, leaving it oddly out of place.

As he raised the cigarette back to his mouth, he momentarily looked away from the mailbox and down to his hands. His fingers were lanky and boney. Little clumps of hair grew around his knuckles and his nails needed cut. Specs of dirt hid under his cuticles.

The chair rocked back and forth as a breeze blew through the porch. Wind chimes hanging from the awning sang their song to deaf ears. A 1940's yellow Chevy truck rusted away under the midday sun off to the side of the house where it had sat in park for longer than anyone could remember. Just as the breeze faded, the mail truck came to a stop in front of the house.

The mailman briefly nodded to Martin when he realized he was being watched. Martin, did not return the nod. The mailman dropped a single envelope in the box, closed it quickly, and drove the truck away.

Martin huffed as he struggled to roll out of his rocking chair. In the process he knocked over the ashtray.

The mailbox was rusting, and he had to pull hard to get it to open. The envelope lay in the center of the metal cell. The box dwarfed the white paper.

Without reading its address, he quickly tore open the envelope, removed the disability check, and stuffed it into the back pocket of his working pants. He crinkled up the envelope and threw it back in the mailbox before slamming the lid shut.

After cleaning up the fallen ashtray, Martin went into his bedroom and collected three extra-large, black garbage bags. He pulled their plastic handles tight to close them, and loaded one over each shoulder, and put the third strap around his neck. It was challenging to breathe with it around his neck, but he didn't have to go far.

Outside, Martin unchained a child's mountain bike from the side of the house. The bike was red and orange and had flames painted on the frame. He had found it sitting with one of his neighbors' garbage bins.

To mount the bike, he had to pull his legs into his chest so they could reach the pedals that were too short for him. After awkwardly shifting the garbage bags' weight around, he pushed off, and into the street.

As he turned off his street, he watched as a group of high school boys played a game of whiffle ball in the park. He started to pedal faster as a few of them turned around toward him. He couldn't make out what they were yelling, but he heard their laughter.

After a ten-minute ride, the light grey shirt he wore had turned dark grey with sweat stains. The flaps of fat that hung over his trousers were doing him no favors. He locked the bike to a light post and walked into the laundromat.

After cashing his check with the cashier, Martin traded a dollar bill for some dimes. The laundromat was empty, except for a middle-aged woman with frizzled red hair and a tremendous overbite that sat in the corner and intensely watched her clothes spin in the washer. He had seen her here before. He wished he could go talk to her.

He found three washers next to each other and separated the stained clothing into the machines. He clicked start and sat down on a bench to watch the clothes spin. He quickly zoned out.

One of the yellow incandescent bulbs that cast a yellow glaze across the laundromat began to flicker and burn out. Martin and the lady with the overbite didn't notice. The laundromat had this terrible beige wallpaper, and the air conditioning was spotty. There were about sixty washers and dryers and about half of them were out of service. An old Chinese man owned the place and played the role of cashier, janitor, electrician, and manager. He wasn't good at fixing things, but he also didn't try very hard.

The washers beeped simultaneously, bringing Martin out of his daydream. He quickly shifted the clothes into the dryers, inserted some more coins, and clicked start. The lady had just left, leaving the Asian man snoring behind the counter, and Martin, dreaming he was somewhere else.

After another spin cycle, the laundry was done, and Martin loaded his garbage bags with the clean clothes. He slung the bags onto his body, unlocked the bike, and pushed off back into the road.

About two minutes away from his house, the garbage bag on Martin's left shoulder split open, letting the clothes fall out. Trying to catch the falling clothing, Martin swerved the bike and lost his balance as he fell onto the asphalt. Two out of the three bags were torn with clothing spread across the street. The road was covered in a thin layer of muddy rainwater, and now too were the clothes.

Without any sign of emotion, Martin collected the now once again dirty clothes into his arms. He pushed the bike off to the side of the road and tossed it into the grass. He walked the rest of the way home.

A father and his son watched on from their porch as Martin struggled to make it up the hill with his arms full of clothes. Martin didn't notice the father's pointing or the son's look of bewilderment.

Pausing at the end of the driveway, Martin opened the mailbox. The crinkled envelope remained where he had left it. He closed the box and set the clothes down on the porch. He turned around to go back for the bike.

The sun was setting, and it was getting colder. He got to the bike and picked it off the grass as the sun dipped below the horizon. He turned the bike back onto the road and began pedaling.

He locked the bike onto the light post outside the laundromat as he had earlier. He opened the door and walked towards the back of the laundromat. It was still empty. He sat down at the bench near the washer in the back-right corner and put some coins in. He pressed start and watched as the water whisked around freely without clothing to impede it.

Something was going to happen. He could feel it.

Work ended at seven in the evening. Randy Sr. usually made it home by ten. Randy Jr. always waited up for his dad.

It was nine o'clock, and tonight, like all other nights, Randy Jr. sat in his pajamas awaiting his father's arrival. The pajamas were light blue and made from a silky material. They had an assortment of superheroes on them. Tonight, he lay sprawled out on the living room couch watching Monday Night Baseball on the small Panasonic TV.

Tonight, Randy Sr. found himself sitting under a bridge, in a beaten-up Pontiac, with a woman he had just paid two hundred dollars sitting in the passenger seat. She had introduced herself as "Emerald," but he had forgotten her alleged name by the time he had taken her top off. He asked if he could call her by his wife's name. Emerald said she didn't mind. And so Emerald, or whatever her real name was, was now Rachael, and she now sat in the backseat of a strange man's car, doing strange things.

At ten o'clock a timer went off in the hooker's bag, and without a word, she departed out of the rear door of the Pontiac. Randy Sr. was left alone in the backseat of his wife's Pontiac, his pants around his ankles, cum drying on his right thigh. It began to rain outside. He climbed over the center console, pulled up his jeans, and buttoned up his ripped flannel. The car started as the rain began to come down harder.

~~~

Randy Sr. was a fifty something year old logger, working and living outside rural Moats County, Washington. Moats Lake was no more than a large pond surrounded by an even smaller town. Home to only one traffic light and some six hundred loggers, there wasn't much to see in Moats. The weather got cold in the winter, and there generally wasn't a spring. The majority of the population was male, and many lived near the poverty line. Logging was a dying industry, and Moats County was proof.

Randy Sr. had six tattoos and two piercings, one in each of his ears. Loggers generally didn't have piercings, and Randy's coworkers were quick to remind him of this. He had gauges in both of his ears, and thus was known at the logging site as 'Gauges.' His hair was grey and overgrown. His facial hair was whiter than it was grey, but it never filled in thick. He kept his hair out of his face with a collection of different hats. Today's light maroon hat read, "Budweiser: America's...," the rest of the tagline had faded off.

He worked six days a week and took overtime hours when they were offered. The work was physically demanding. The logging turnover rate was high, but those that lived in Moats County specifically rarely quit. There weren't many other jobs to be had in Moats. Few people ever left the place. Something kept people there longer than anyone could ever understand.

He spent his day off preparing to restart the work week. He cleaned his tools, washed his boots, and caught up on sleep. Work paid the bills, but more importantly, it kept him busy. It was the kind of work that kept his mind from doing too much wandering.

Randy Jr. wanted the kind of dad he saw in movies. He wanted bedtime stories and fishing lessons. He wanted a dad to take him to baseball games.

Twelve years old, he lingered at an awkward age. He knew, deep down, that he deserved more from his father, yet he remained innocently hopeful that his father would be the hero he wanted him to be.

He understood too much to remain innocent to his father's lack of interest in him, yet he was too young to fully grasp what it was that was driving his father away. Naturally, he blamed himself for his father's lack of love.

Although he looked like his mother, he retained his father's nose and bad teeth. He was bulky for his age and his wide shoulders made his physique look defined through t-shirts. He didn't say much, but when he did, he talked slowly and thought carefully before speaking. He raked leaves in the fall and walked dogs in the summer to provide for himself. His father often didn't have the money to buy his son the things he needed.

He didn't like school, but there wasn't much to do at home either. He had already lost the few friends he had been able to make. Most of the boys had stopped attending school to start shadowing their fathers at the logging sites.

He didn't remember his mother. He wished he had just a few memories of her. Just being able to remember what she sounded like would've been enough. He didn't like to talk about it.

Randy Sr. had told his son that his mom died in a car crash. This is what Randy Jr. believed to be true. Sometimes so did his dad. This was not true though. She had killed herself. She jumped off a bridge.

~~~

Randy Sr. opened up the accelerator and moved the Pontiac out from under the bridge and into the rain. It was now ten thirty. He considered making a stop at his favorite bar, but decided against it when he remembered he wouldn't get paid for another week. He turned the Pontiac onto the freeway and toward home. He tried to clear the thoughts from his mind as he drove. The roads were empty. He set the cruise control and leaned back into the brown vinyl.

When he pulled into the driveway at quarter past eleven, it was raining quite hard. He brought the Pontiac to a stop in front of the garage door and put it in park. He grabbed yesterday's paper from under the passenger seat and put it above his head to shield himself from the rain as he locked the car and ran up the stairs of the house. The door was rusted and stuck as he pulled it open.

The house was a small duplex, but the second side had been vacant for years. There were brown shutters and a green awning. The wooden porch in front of Randy's unit was falling apart. Some of the windows in the vacant unit were shattered and the light grey gutter was hanging off the left side of the roof.

Randy pushed the screen door open and set the wet newspaper down on the kitchen table. He walked into the kitchen and took the coffee pot out from under the sink. He plugged it in and poured a decaf blend into the top of the machine.

The TV was on in the living room and Randy Jr. was sleeping face down on the couch. Randy Sr. lifted him off the couch and turned him over to lay on his back. He pulled a blanket off the recliner and laid it on top of his son. His son was wearing a baseball glove on his left hand. The glove had a ball inside it. In his right hand, he had a small piece of paper clenched in his fist.

Randy Sr. took the glove, which used to be his, and set it on the coffee table next to the couch. He carefully pried the piece of paper from his son's hand without waking him.

In ugly, black block letters the note read, "Dad, can you teach me to play catch this weekend?" Above this sentence there were other words and sentences that had been crossed out.

Randy Sr. took the paper into the kitchen, poured a cup of coffee, and threw the note in the garbage can.

Poems:
*** *indicates poem continued on next page*

Empty, Ohio, 2020

where am i

she moves like
tree branches blown by fall wind
somewhere between grace and distress
barely holding on

but
always for
you
your amusement

and you clap
lightheartedly
throwing a dollar on the stage
now and again

and she gets off the stage
and leans into you
her bare tits
in your face
and says something

but you aren't listening
even those
voluptuous tits
can't bring you back
to the present

so she gets back on the stage
reclaims her domain
and resumes her sensual ways
***

and you look up
and now she is gone
it is time to close things down
the club can't be open
any longer

not even
for you

and finally
you look around
and wonder
how long you've been there

a glimpse into the past

it's winter and
it's cold and dark out
after all

i certainly didn't want to be cold and
i don't like cups with coins
rattling in my face
and neither do you
but for different reasons

neither of us add coins to the cup
the interaction over
you depart
and so do i

but before i leave
i lean into his ear
and put my face against
his grimy beard

i can feel the dirt
mixed with greasy hair and cigarette smoke
and i whisper

we pause
both of us
trying to understand what i said
and why

i take my face out of
the grime
and he looks at me***

i know he recognizes me

on adventures (and adventuring)

it started with what we referred to as a
"wrong" turn
as they so often do
both metaphorically
and literally

we ventured on
down this "wrong" road
to our "wrong" destination
unintended and unforeseen

supposedly headed for the country
we emerged out of a long tunnel
along the coastline

it was 5:06pm
the wedding ceremony had started
some six minutes ago

i turned to my husband
of five years
we too had been married
in the early evening of a
fall saturday
in the country outside
san pedro

he turned to me
sitting in the passenger seat
with his black suit and tie
***

i shrugged
and turned to the sea
extending without limit
in front of our red
chevy

it was ours
since his father passed away
and it ran well
for two hundred thousand miles

the old man drove the thing nearly
all his life
back and forth
mostly from his farm
to town
and back again

we had gotten married on that farm
some five years ago
on a fall saturday
in the country
outside san pedro

but now we were late
to another wedding
another union of love
out in the country
and the truck just seemed
awfully content
sitting on the edge of those
black sea cliffs
descending into the pacific
***

and so
i put it in park and
turned off the engine

the sun had started its descent
but still had some work left
to fall below and
drop off the edge of the table
into the sea

i don't think it had ever seen
a black tie day
in its life
that red chevy pickup truck

until today

i took the pins out of my hair
and changed the heels for boots
my husband
his tie already loosened
top button undone
and suit coat
left in the passenger seat

coming around the back of the flatbed
he took my hands
not so differently
than the way he had
some five years ago
and led me
in my black dress
to the edge of the cliffs
***

and we stood there for awhile
just standing
saying nothing
just watching
listening
until we walked down
down some untrodden path
leading to tidal pools on the edge of
that great blue monster
and we climbed all the way down
until we just sat there
sat there
in these tidal pools
at the edge of the pacific
far down a "wrong" road
following a "wrong" turn
and we got in
we sat ourselves
fully clothed
black tie
in those tidal pools
as the water washed up onto us
and as the sun dipped below the horizon
a light rain
not much more than a mist
began to fall
making our tidal pools
just a little bit
deeper
as the light on the horizon
slowly faded
and turned to
darkness

holding onto it

i wonder if she realizes
i'm using her to write
my poems

in the moment
i'm not
i don't think
after all
i'm present
with her
mostly

perhaps i smirk
or chuckle
when i realize
something we did
or something she said
was poetic
bound for the lined paper
in my leather notebook

but really
there's nothing wrong with
finding the beauty in this world
and holding onto it
so you can keep it
in your notebook

too bad
not even my notebook
can hold onto her

reflections

there are so many
forgotten places
for me
to caress a glass
and sip its innards
to find the words for my next
poem

but these days
the words have stopped coming

i look under my glass
i look in my glass
they aren't there

must just call for
another round
under the yellow hue
of cheap lights
and dull conversation
in a dirty
basement bar
with ripped high top seats
that reek of those wanting more

i just know
i know
one more drink
will bring those words
back
***

so i wave down the bartender
he knows my name
he knows my drink
and he moves to refill my glass
and the mirror behind the bar
is reflecting some image

i don't recognize him
the bartender puts the drink down in front
of him
he doesn't move
he's just staring at me

this seems poetic
but the words do not come

when you were young
in this matter
there was never
any question
any doubt

a lover
a friend
anyone
someone
would be there

but now
you are old
and doubt has crept past
the horizon
grasping for something to latch onto
and someone is banging
on the stall door
in that public bathroom
outside Encino

and with a horrible noise
you wretch one more time
leaving your insides in the rusted porcelain

and now
there is no one there
to hold your hair

sometimes i have revelations on the subway

the train did not wait for me
which left me waiting
long enough
to look around

one hundred feet above
it was dark
and the snow was beginning to fall
the streetlamps were turning on
coffee brewing
fireplaces being lit
order restored

but down below
another story unfolds
a story not meant for
my eyes
after all
i should have been on the train

and i never should have seen the man
in the torn jacket
climbing onto the subway tracks
and walking into the tunnel
with a metal flask and
a smile years removed
looking for a warm place to sleep
***

but just then
before he disappeared
into the darkness
that old smile
rusted and broken
came back
and it was subtle
so subtle
that most would've
missed it

and i know
he was happier

than i could ever be

the train is coming
this isn't my stop

a problem

you have a problem
is what she said to me
when i vomited
in the backseat
of a taxi
on the way home
from my son's baseball game

why not
have a few
drinks
in the bleachers
of my son's ball game

it's just like being at the ballpark
watching the pros
really
if you think about it
they sell drinks there
at the professional games
right
***

except
i was the only one drinking
and the parents were staring
and telling me
to sit down
and be quiet
and my son's coach told me
to leave
and my son
got taken out of the game
because he was crying
uncontrollably
in center field

you can't catch a flyball
when you are crying uncontrollably
after all

but how dare she
tell me
i have a problem
me, having the problem

no
you have the problem
said me
and every
drunk
to vomit
in the backseat
of a taxi
coming home from their son's baseball game

july

it doesn't get hot here in july anymore
something about global warming
i'm not sure
i never did well in science class

i used to drink
to cool off
pack a few beers in a cooler
with some ice

to refresh myself
after a few hours
on the site
welding was demanding work
after all
just ask anyone

but now it is july
again
and it is not hot
and i am not parched
and my mug
is filled with
cheap vodka
and i tell myself
it's to keep me warm

getting stuck
in a life
habits
consistency
the good life
the comfortable life
with the picket fence
to keep them out
and you
in

it makes me fear
fretting for my own sanity

but how pitiful
to fear your own destruction
at the hands of a fence

to fear
for yourself
so fucking disgusting

when children are blowing bubbles
and friends are getting cancer
and your neighbor is stabbing his wife
and the grass is growing
how absolutely absurd
to fear
my own death
at the hands
of that goddamn
fence

no easy way to tell the truth, so we make things up

it was rather silly
but the thunder
used to frighten me
i couldn't comprehend
why the sky was
banging
i couldn't foresee a reason for it
to be upset

we were all surely
going to die
by its might
for who could fight the sky
and win

and my mother
got quite concerned
as good mothers
do
seeing her little baby
curled up
with a blanket over his head

and she would say
don't be scared
that's just your grandpa
up in heaven
bowling another strike
and knocking down the pins
***

this settled me
and in truth
it settled her
too
it even made me
smile
during the storms
it was just grandpa
he wasn't scary

but one night
during a terrible
storm
something occurred to me

grandpa used to bowl
a few times a week
when he was
alive

why would he only bowl
once every few weeks
when a terrible storm
passed through
now that he was in heaven

i couldn't imagine
god limited your bowling privileges
in heaven
that would defeat the whole purpose of heaven
if you couldn't bowl
when you wanted
***

and something became clear that night

nobody knows why
the sky rumbles

we all just find
some excuse
to comfort us

and for my grandpa
he was not in some
heavenly bowling alley
no
his coffin
lay in a cemetery
no more than
five miles
from where i currently sit
and his body
is in that
wooden box

and that box
is four feet under dirt
and it is next to
another box
with some other dead person in it
and that person isn't bowling either
because they are in
a box
next to my grandpa
four feet under dirt
dead
and you can't be bowling strikes***

when you're dead

portrait of a porch

the cars sit half amputated
on browning grass
of an old lady's
property

they are now her cars
it is now her property
that is now her husband buried under the conifer tree
behind the house

sunlight strips through an early morning's
fog
and brightens the cobalt rust
on the three cars sitting
on their cement slabs

a gust of wind sends the chimes
on the porch
into fury
she pulls the quilt higher
to cover her neck

it's quiet there
except for the chimes
no one left in the town
no one in her home

he used to mine there
like the rest of them
until they finally
learned
about the radiation***

and now the ones left
moved
or died
cancer
mostly
prolonged exposure

but not her
she stayed
couldn't leave
this is where he wanted
to be

and so

her chair still rocks
back and forth
creaking a bit
these days

as the three cars in front of her porch
still rust more

at the edge of the world

northern canada is where we were
and i mean real
north
the kind of north you can't drive to
because
there aren't any roads

real north
like
take a plane north

and that's what we did
my father and i
nothing more than a four seater
we took that plane up
to northern canada

we each carried a
eighty liter pack
nearly filled
likely
far more than we should've been carrying
no doubt
worsening
the back problems my father had
and the ones
i would discover
some thirty years later
***

and we each carried
one rifle
i don't recall
the make or model

i never hunted much
after that trip

but there we were
waving goodbye
as the four seater
seaplane
took off
and left us
alone
on that small lake
in northern canada
destined to return in seven days' time
when we and our supplies
would be diminished

and we did it
what we came there to do
in that week
we killed the one
moose
the one
that my father had applied for
and been allotted
approved to kill
with our rifles
and our piece of paper
that said
we could kill it***

and then
we mostly just sat there
on the edge of that lake
and depleted the food we had brought

and as the carcass grew smellier
we kept it intact
and hung it in a tree
so the animals wouldn't get to it

the taxidermist would struggle with it
but he made it work
i forget what happened to it
the body
after the taxidermist
returned it

and then
some seven days later
the seaplane arrived back
landing just where it had been
a week ago

and we loaded the body
and our packs
into the back of the plane

and flew south
very far south
out and away from a very northern part
of northern canada
and to this day
i doubt anyone
has returned to that lake

poetry

i just don't get it
is what they mutter
the words, the phrases
the goddamn literary devices

what is poetry

why
teacher
do you make us spend hours
pouring over nonsense
that you make us believe
makes sense

how do you know
its meaning

what if you're wrong
what if it's all just black words
on white paper

to that i respond
you couldn't be more right
it's all a bunch of crap
crap words on a shit page
and it means a whole
lot
of
nothing

but goddamnit if it isn't
beautiful

storage facility

today i left
i really left
all my things
in a storage facility
you know
one of those big garages
where people hide things
from themselves
things they will
soon forget

today i left
everyone who has ever
met me
hoping to never see them
again
i wish they also made
a big garage
to store them in
but someone told me
that was inhumane

today i left
my job
oh that great killer
taking my soul
a bit more every day
every report due
every meeting to sit in on
i don't need a storage facility for that
i need a fucking fire
***

today i left
my sensibilities
and my fears
and my dreams
or what i thought
were dreams
and i got them
altogether
and i
deleted them
no fire
nor
storage facility
required

tomorrow i renew
a membership
with no monthly dues
and 0% APR
whatever that stands for
to this thing we call
living

and i can't fucking wait

untitled

i used to think
that if i was sitting by the window
and my drink was steaming
making the glass fog
pen in hand
and it began to rain
a great poem was coming

but now the rain doesn't come
my drink has gone cold
and i have nowhere to run

i'm no writer
i haven't even
lived one life
over
who am i
to recount
life
to you

now i know why i became a writer

can you help me?

the days are getting shorter

do you ever wonder
why the trees
have grooves
or
why the birds
sing
when there are no other birds
to hear

or why water
puddles
and hearts
break

no
i imagine you don't consider
these things
when the divorce papers
need filing
and custody
needs determined

and for the trees
in case you were wondering
the squirrels need the grooves
to climb

but you weren't wondering
i know that much

is there more

a brief visit
lasts longer
than she wants
and shorter than i prefer

i'd love to reacquaint
i tell her
but she says
it simply
isn't possible

there is no more here
nothing more to be had
our story
penned thoughtfully
has been erased
prematurely
a story told in love songs
never to be sung
again
because you had to leave
without even
a word

searching for meaning in a place like this

is like fishing without a pole
cleaning a chimney
with a toothbrush

futile

it will only lead
to a slow
and steady
burn

a spark's
sudden light
hope

but then
you leave it
alone
crackling
burning
fading
and soon
the light goes out
and the story is over
and the air is flying by
it has a mustiness
to it

and nothing
could be
darker

a momentary lapse in time

the things that can be learned
from a simple
sideways glance
are like the things
you hear in rumors
hushed tones telling things
they should not know
so fleeting
but
they must be true
they must mean something
or so
you think

or else
why would she have sent you
that glance
from across the room
it certainly wasn't
an accident

how a quick
sideways glance
is like a shadow
cast upon the lamp shade
of a lamp
that won't turn on
in a penthouse far above the streets
far away from the cries of a city
wanting to tell its tales
in the shadows
***

how a glance can spark
a life
between lovers
finding solace
in a brief moment
forever ruining their chances
of being alone

rivers, far too poetic

it's sunday
and i've told mother i'm feeling sick
and i can't
go to church

and i think she knows
i'm lying
but today
she can't
play my games
she's exhausted
hardly slept
even i don't notice
the cut below her lip

and so i'm here
alone
in the four room tudor

a light rain drizzling
i decide to leave
and find adventure

there's a stream down the road
and my fishing pole in the garage
and the water is high
***

so i cast
and
my line waffles
a bit
in the stream
i lift my glasses
and peer into the water
the rain drops are pounding
there's a boy looking back at me
he seems small
scared
i don't recognize him

a fish bites my line
the boy leaves

there's beauty in disappearing

i found her in the mountains
off some back road
an old house
turned inn

she built it with her husband
some twenty years ago
mostly with stone

and she showed me into the kitchen
to an old mahogany wood table
chipped and stained
and sturdy

the fridge was broke
so beers were served warm
and we began talking

we talked
at first
of the mundane
getting the easy stuff
out of the way

but the easy stuff
lasted awhile
and it was getting late
and she was about to leave

but then
something happened
***

we started
really talking

the things
you wouldn't tell
a stranger

the things
you don't even talk to
yourself
about

but there we were
sitting around that mahogany table
telling of fears
losses
dreams
loves

and we all knew

we would never be back
to that inn
we would never come back
to those mountains
we would never see each other
again

and that
was what mattered

Please Be Quiet, Ohio, 2020

At the time of this publication, Bobby is a 21-year-old undergraduate student at the University of Michigan, pursuing a dual major in business and UX/UI Design. Born and raised in the suburbs of Cleveland, Ohio, Bobby has a love for creating. He created his own photo/video media production company at the age of 17 and has been writing creatively for as long as he can remember. At the time of this publication, Bobby just finished revising his first feature length screenplay, a project he undertook with his go-to adventure and creative projects counterpart, Noah Jacobs.

Bobby believes in the power of stories as a means to help make humans more empathetic, understanding, and motivated to make change. When he's not creating, you might find him backpacking in the wilderness, chasing breaking news as an aspiring journalist, consuming everything he can related to entrepreneurship and startups, watching Wes Anderson movies, scuba diving, or attending a music festival or concert.

Bobby wants to hear from you! Reach out to:
Tell him what you thought of his work
Read more of his work
Read his 90-page feature length movie script
Work together on a photo/video project
Buy any of his photographs seen in this book
Help him sell his movie script or new books
Hire him
Philosophize
Go on an adventure

Bobby Housel:
440-221-8719
bhousel9@hotmail.com
Scan below QR Code for all of Bobby's online socials

The End, A Store in Rural Ohio/Amish Country, 2020

Made in the USA
Las Vegas, NV
21 August 2022

53720718R00069